BEST ~IN~ SHOW

Karen LeFrak
illustrated by Andrew Day

Walker & Company **New York**

ACKNOWLEDGMENTS

Trophies and ribbons go to my extraordinary publisher and editor, Emily Easton;
wonderful literary agent, Frederica Friedman; talented illustrator, Andrew Day;
mentor and friend, Wendell Sammet; friends T. Byram Karasu and David Kahn;
husband, Richard LeFrak; and all delightful poodles everywhere.
—K. L.

First published in the United States of America in February 2011
by Walker Publishing Company, Inc., a division of Bloomsbury Publishing, Inc.
www.bloomsburykids.com

For information about permission to reproduce selections from this book, write to
Permissions, Walker BFYR, 175 Fifth Avenue, New York, New York 10010

Library of Congress Cataloging-in-Publication Data
LeFrak, Karen.
Best in Show / Karen LeFrak ; illustrated by Andrew Day. — 1st U.S. ed.
p.   cm.
Summary: Abby is convinced that Gem, a poodle puppy, will grow up to be a champion, and helps with her
grooming and training to make sure that will happen—which comes in handy when Gem's trainer is injured
the day of the big show. Includes "Infurmation" about dog shows and poodles.
ISBN 978-0-8027-2064-1 (hardcover) • ISBN 978-0-8027-2065-8 (reinforced)
[1. Dog shows—Fiction. 2. Dogs—Training—Fiction. 3. Poodles—Fiction. 4. Animals—Infancy—Fiction.]
I. Day, Andrew. II. Title.
PZ7.L5211144Bes 2011   [E]—dc22   2010010330

Art created using variations of pencils, ranging from the lightest graphite
to the darkest, then colored with watercolor washes
Typeset in Humana Sans Medium
Book design by Donna Mark

Printed in China by C&C Offset Printing Co., Ltd., Shenzhen, Guangdong
2 4 6 8 10 9 7 5 3 1 (hardcover)
2 4 6 8 10 9 7 5 3 1 (reinforced)

All papers used by Bloomsbury Publishing, Inc., are natural, recyclable products
made from wood grown in well-managed forests. The manufacturing processes
conform to the environmental regulations of the country of origin.

To "Mikimoto," the grandest champion of them all!
—K. L.

To Mom, for always having my back
—A. D.

"**H**ere's our next Best in Show winner," Abby announced as she cuddled the little pup. Her dog Jewel had just delivered a litter of five puppies. "I think I'll call her Gem. Her white coat sparkles like a diamond."

"That's a perfect name for one of Jewel's pups," said Wendell, the handler and kennel owner.

The next afternoon, Abby couldn't wait to visit Gem.
　　She'd loved Standard Poodles ever since her aunt Nancy, the kennel keeper, gave her a stuffed pink poodle for her sixth birthday.

"Now that you're old enough, would you like
to help with the pups?" asked Aunt Nancy.
"Abso-poodley!" said Abby,
jumping with joy.

Abby watched the pups grow bigger every day. After two weeks, their eyes and ears opened, and they piled on top of each other in a big puppy pile to stay warm and cozy.

A few weeks later,
they tumbled their way
over to their water bowl
and around their pen.

At eight weeks, Abby and Aunt Nancy painted the pups' tails with food coloring to tell them apart. Gem's tail looked like pink cotton candy.

"I know Gem will be a champion show dog someday," Abby stated proudly. "Just look at how her tail never stops wagging. She's the pick of the litter."

"We'll have to wait and see," said Wendell.

Could Gem really be a show dog someday?

Once Gem turned twelve weeks old, it was time to find out.

First, Abby studied how Wendell put a special show leash, called a lead, on Gem and walked her around at a slow and steady pace, called a gait. When Wendell stopped, Gem stopped too. She could even "follow the bait"—watching as Wendell moved a treat from side to side.

Gem was definitely show-dog material.

Now they had work to do. Over the next few months, Gem practiced and started competing at small shows in the poodle puppy classes in "Puppy" trim. Sometimes she won a ribbon, and other times a different poodle won instead. A black poodle from England named Cheerio was her toughest competition.

"It's important to be a good loser *and* a good winner," said Wendell after he congratulated Cheerio's handler.

Abby wasn't convinced though. She wanted everyone else to love Gem just as much as she did.

Finally in "Grown-up" trim, Gem earned enough ribbons to be a champion and qualify for the grandest dog show all year.

The day of the big show, Abby helped Gem get puffed and fluffed.

First, it was bath time, with lots of shampoo to make Gem's hair white and shiny.

Next, her hair was dried with a giant hair blower.

Then Wendell snipped her fur with special scissors. Abby thought the bracelets on Gem's legs looked like giant marshmallows.

To top it all off, her mane was swept up with pink elastic bands and protected until showtime with pink plastic wrappers that looked like curlers.

Gem looked perfect.

"Good luck, and bring home lots of ribbons!" shouted Aunt Nancy as Wendell and Abby drove off to the show.

When they arrived, the show site, bustling with activity, amazed Abby.

Wendell and Abby quickly found the poodle ring and began to get Gem ready for her big moment. Everywhere Abby looked, owners petted and primped their dogs.

"Oh no!" said Abby. "I forgot the pin brush for Gem's tail."

"Don't worry," Wendell said. "We may compete seriously in the ring, but we're all friends in the grooming area. Someone will lend you a brush."

Abby sighed with relief as Cheerio's owner helped them out.

Abby found her seat just in time for the Best of Breed judging. The stands were filled with dog lovers. Cheerio and her owner went first. She looked beautiful, but Abby thought Gem looked better.

When it was Gem's turn to gait, Abby held her breath. She
thought Wendell and Gem looked wonderful as they moved
together around the enormous ring. The judge agreed and gave
Wendell the ribbon for Best of Breed.

That night, Gem entered the ring again, this time to compete in the Best in Non-Sporting Group judging.

But as Wendell turned the corner, something terrible happened. His shoe skidded on the slippery green carpet. The crowd gasped as he fell. Abby held her breath, and Gem stood very still as Wendell got up slowly.

"Come along, Gem," he whispered. Even though Gem's lead broke in the fall, she followed rhythmically beside Wendell as he limped around the ring.

The crowd cheered. Gem had never behaved better.

Abby tried not to worry as the contest continued. The judge ran his hand across Gem's back, and her tail danced like a feather duster. When he bent down to stroke her chest, Gem licked his cheek. The judge couldn't help but smile.

Then he rewarded Gem and Wendell with a big blue ribbon.

Gem had won Best in Group. Now she could compete for Best in Show!

But Wendell's leg was still hurt. How could Gem ever win Best in Show if Wendell couldn't take her around the ring? Gem had worked too hard to miss her big moment.

Abby leaned in nose-to-nose with Gem and said, "You deserve to show them what you can do!"

Wendell put a new lead on Gem and said, "Abby, I need you to take Gem into the ring. You've practiced enough, and she loves you. Just do your best and she will do *her* best."

Gem and Abby bounced into the ring. Gem pranced, posed, and performed perfectly. And the crowd was on their side too.

"Poo-dle! Poo-dle!" everyone shouted as Gem and Abby circled the ring.

Once his decision was made, the Best in Show judge quieted the crowd. He called, "Let me have the Standard Poodle, please."

Abby raised her arms with joy, and Gem jumped right into them.
She had known all along that Gem was the pick of the litter.

INFURMATION

Would you ever want to show a dog, like Abby showed Gem?
You can be a junior handler in a real dog show when you are nine.

What would you look for if you were a judge?
You would look for the poodle's head to be up like it's proud, the tail to be up like a lollipop, a straight back, and a steady, springy gait.

Do you know why poodles like Gem have such fancy haircuts?
Poodles used to help hunters find ducks in the water. Fur shaped like pom-poms or puffs kept the poodle's hips and ankles warm. Bare legs made it easier to swim. Until one year of age, a poodle can be shown in a "Puppy" trim. After that, it is shown in either Continental or English Saddle trim.

Do poodles come in different sizes?
Yes—big ones like Gem and Cheerio are called Standards, medium-sized poodles are called Miniatures, and small ones are called Toys.

How many different kinds of dogs are there?
There are more than 150 different breeds. Each is a member of one of the seven groups, including Non-Sporting (Gem's group), Sporting, Hound, Working, Terrier, Herding, and Toy.

Would you like to go to a dog show?
Dog shows take place every weekend throughout the year. To find one near your home, you can get in touch with the American Kennel Club, or visit its Web site at www.akc.org.